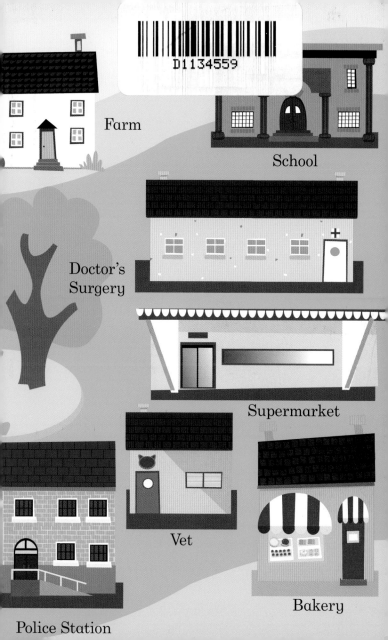

Farm

School

Doctor's
Surgery

Supermarket

Vet

Bakery

Police Station

A catalogue record for this book is available from the British Library

Published by Ladybird Books Ltd

80 Strand London WC2R ORL

A Penguin Company

1 3 5 7 9 10 8 6 4 2

ISBN: 978-1-40930-290-2

Printed in China

Just the Job
Doris the Doctor

by Mandy Ross
illustrated by Paul Nicholls

Doris the doctor got up early one morning. "It's Healthy Heart Day today," she said, and off she went for a healthy run before breakfast.

Doris ate a very healthy breakfast. "Mustn't forget my stethoscope," she said as she set off for work. "I'll be listening to lots of hearts today."

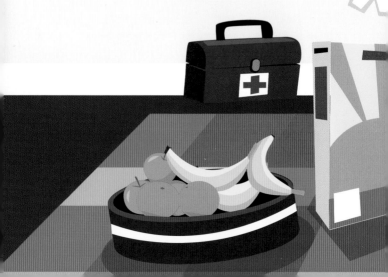

9

Story Town Surgery
was busy. Lots of people
had come for a Healthy
Heart check-up.

The first patient was
Frank the farmer.
His heart sounded
very healthy.
Ba-doum! Ba-doum!
"Do you get lots of exercise?"
asked Doris. "Exercise is
good for hearts."

13

"Plenty,"
said Frank,
"chasing cows!"

The next patient was
Violet the vet. Her heart
sounded very healthy, too.
Ba-doum! Ba-doum!
"Do you get lots
of exercise?"
asked Doris.

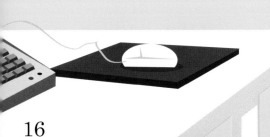

"Plenty," said Violet,
"chasing naughty dogs!"

19

The last patient that day
was Ben the builder. But his
heart sounded very strange.
Eeek! Eeek! Eeek!
"Do you get lots of...
MOUSE!" shouted Doris.

HEALTHY

HEA
DA

21

Suddenly, Ben's pet mouse
jumped out of his shirt
pocket and down onto
the floor.
"Eeek!" shrieked Doris.

23

Ben chased the mouse
all round the surgery.
At last he caught it.
"I can see you get
LOTS of exercise,"
said Doris.
"Plenty," said
Ben, "chasing
this mouse!"

HEALTHY

HEART
DAY

25

Then Doris had
another go at listening
to Ben's heart.

Ba-doum! Ba-doum!
"That sounds like a
very healthy heart!"
said Doris.

When she got home for her tea, Doris the doctor found a heart-shaped card on her doorstep. Inside it said,

Thanks for looking after our hearts, Doris.

Ben x

Violet x

Frank x

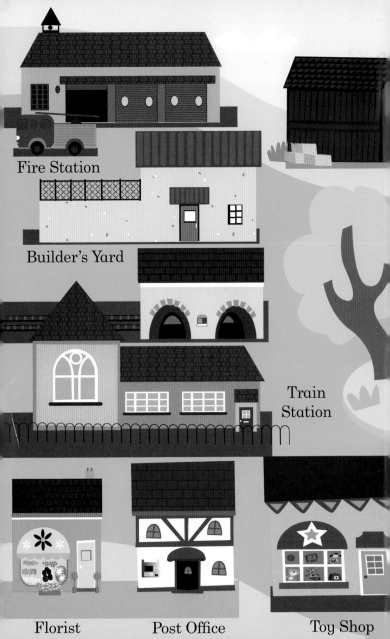

Fire Station

Builder's Yard

Train
Station

Florist

Post Office

Toy Shop